CRAFTS
OF THE MIDDLE AGES™

THE CRAFTS AND CULTURE OF A
MEDIEVAL TOWN

Joann Jovinelly and Jason Netelkos

rosen
central™

For Mom, a spirited and creative woman who taught me it was possible to make magic

Published in 2007 by The Rosen Publishing Group, Inc.
29 East 21st Street, New York, NY 10010

First Edition

Library of Congress Cataloging-in-Publication Data

Jovinelly, Joann.
The crafts and culture of a Medieval town / Joann Jovinelly and Jason Netelkos.—1st ed.
      p. cm.—(The crafts and culture of the Middle Ages)
Includes index.
ISBN 1-4042-0761-9 (library binding)
1. Handicraft—Europe—History—To 1500—Juvenile literature. 2. Cities and towns—Europe—History—To 1500—Juvenile literature. 3. Middle Ages—Europe—History—Juvenile literature. I. Netelkos, Jason. II. Title. III. Series: Jovinelly, Joann. Crafts and culture of the Middle Ages.
TT55.J68 2007
940.1—dc22

                                                                    2005029162

Manufactured in the United States of America

Note to parents
Some of these projects require tools or materials that can be dangerous if used improperly. Adult supervision will be necessary for projects that require the use of a craft knife, an oven, a stove top, or pins and needles. Before starting any of the projects in this book, you may want to cover your work area with newspaper or plastic. In addition, we recommend using a piece of thick cardboard to protect surfaces while cutting with craft or mat knives. We encourage you to discuss safety with your children and note in advance which projects may require your supervision.

CONTENTS

The term "Middle Ages" refers to the approximately 1,000-year period in western Europe from about AD 500 to 1500. That period coincides roughly with the collapse of the Western Roman Empire and the beginnings of the Renaissance in the fifteenth century.

The collapse of the western empire in the fifth century brought an end to several centuries of Roman rule in western Europe. During that period, Rome constituted the sole political, social, and economic authority uniting diverse peoples in regions that include the present-day countries of England, France, Spain, Italy, Germany, and Portugal. The Rhine and Danube rivers roughly marked the northern and eastern frontiers of the western

The medieval city of Augsburg, in present-day Germany, is featured in this detail of a woodcut from the Nuremberg Chronicle *(1493), by Hartman Schedel.*

empire. Beyond those frontiers were the lands of the Germanic and Slavic peoples of the rest of Europe—the "barbarians" as the Romans collectively regarded them.

Troubled by corruption, internal political strife, civil war, and epidemics, the western empire found it increasingly difficult to defend its borders against these barbarians, particularly the Goths. By the end of the fifth century, the barbarians had overrun the empire, and the Goths had even invaded and sacked Rome itself.

As the Roman system fragmented into competing political and economic kingdoms, western Europe became unstable. When the Middle Ages began, the lands and peoples of the old Roman Empire came under constant pressure in the form of invasion. Germanic peoples from the east such as the Goths, Franks, Lombards, Vandals, Angles, and Saxons continued to ravage the region. From the north, along the Atlantic, fearsome seafaring raiders from Scandinavia—the Vikings—also plundered the castles and monasteries along European coastlines.

Simultaneously, invaders from the Middle East and North Africa, armed with the new religion of Islam, approached from the south and west. Muslim warriors conquered much of the Iberian and Balkan peninsulas before their European advance was temporarily halted.

The old systems of Roman trade and military protection were disrupted in the turmoil. It seemed as if the light of Roman civilization had been extinguished, plunging the former empire into darkness. The early centuries of the Middle Ages are sometimes referred to as the Dark Ages for this reason.

UNIFYING FORCES

Amid the chaos of the Middle Ages, several unifying forces did emerge. Among these, the most important was Roman Catholicism. By the time of the fall of the empire, Christianity

The Germanic Kingdoms and the East Roman Empire in 526

This map of Europe in 526 shows the emerging Germanic kingdoms of the early Middle Ages. After the breakup of the Roman Empire in the west, various groups dominated the region, such as the Franks, Goths, and Vandals.

had become its official religion. At the start of the Middle Ages, western Europe was overwhelmingly Roman Catholic. Latin, which was the language of the empire and the language of worship of Roman Catholicism, survived in western Europe for centuries.

Roman Catholicism dominated every aspect of life in the Middle Ages. For the European of that time, there was no distinction between the secular and the religious. Over time, everything from the overall organization of society to the everyday behavior of individuals came to be understood in terms of the human being's relationship with God.

The way society was organized, for example, was believed to rest on divine authority. Political and legal power was divine power, and vice versa. This does not mean that the people of the Middle Ages regarded their rulers as being divine, but they did regard whatever power their rulers exercised as being divinely sanctioned. The society of the Middle Ages was one in which the various kingdoms were ultimately united by their shared Catholic faith and the loyalty to the pope that it demanded. Loyalty to the church continued despite the ceaseless competition, strife, and warfare among these new divisions.

As the head of the Roman Catholic Church, the pope in the Middle Ages was a political leader as much as a religious leader. In theory, at least, the pope was regarded as receiving his authority directly from God. Although he might have had few armies at his direct command and relatively small territory under his control, the pope still possessed tremendous power. Society under the pope was organized downward in descending positions of obedience to his ultimate authority. People believed God wanted it that way.

The society of the Middle Ages was generally a feudal society. The states that emerged were ruled by a monarch, generally a king. The great majority of the people lived in the countryside, rather than in cities, and earned their living from agriculture, rather than business or trade. Very few people would have owned the land on which they lived and worked, however. Property was owned by the small, privileged class known as the nobility.

The nobility allowed the peasants, as the landless masses were known, to live on and work the land in exchange for the peasants' loyalty. In theory, the nobles were also to provide the peasants with protection and defense against outside invaders. The peasants were similarly obligated to provide than simply defiance against society's conventions or breaking the law. It was seen as a sin against God. It was this view of the world that helped give the pope such power. A king might defy or disobey the pope, but he did so at the peril of his soul, for the pope could excommunicate him, or expel him from the church. The excommunicated person, even a king, was outside of any legal protection or obligation of loyalty or obedience. Even worse, his soul was consigned to eternal damnation.

TOWNS AND CITIES

By about AD 1000, western Europe had been revitalized in many ways. The various Germanic peoples had largely established themselves in new lands across the former Roman Empire, most notably in what are today France (the Franks), England (the Angles and the Saxons), and Italy (the Lombards, Goths, and Vandals). Western Europe developed greater stability and prosperity as new political institutions were established. (The establishment of the Frankish kingdoms around AD 800 in what is now France and the creation of the Holy Roman Empire are two examples.) Increased stability and the development of new farming techniques (such as the plow and construction of dams) led to larger harvests and increased

Pope Boniface VIII is featured declaring his papal laws in this fourteenth-century manuscript titled Decrees of Boniface VIII. *Christian doctrines determined the laws during the Middle Ages.*

military or other service to the nobles when needed. The nobles' right to their land, in turn, was derived from the king; similar mutual obligations of loyalty, defense, and service bound the king and his nobles. Also, in theory, mutual obligations of loyalty and service bound the kings of Europe to the pope. The church also had its own nobility, the bishops, who were awarded control of large landholdings. A person was born into either the peasantry or the nobility. There was virtually no way to move between the classes.

Failure to fulfill obligations under the feudal systems was viewed as more population. Indeed, by about 1250, Europe's population was at the highest level it would be for many centuries. In turn, such stability allowed western Europe to defend itself better against the likes of the Vikings and the Muslims. By the eleventh century, the Catholic Church's popes were even feeling secure enough to call on Europe's kings to mount "crusades" to liberate the Christian holy lands of the Middle East from their Muslim conquerors. This increased prosperity both fed off and was stimulated by another important development: the widespread growth of towns and cities in western Europe.

As farming techniques improved, fewer peasants were needed to work the European countryside. Many of these former peasants migrated to towns where they became merchants. Merchants sold their wares in the towns' weekly markets as well as at trade fairs great distances away. Merchants from various towns and cities traveled to one location to trade or purchase goods over a forty-nine-day period. Some of these medieval fairs,

such as those of Champagne, France, were famous throughout Europe. In times of good international relations, merchants from North Africa, Russia, Scandinavia, and the Middle East would be present. Nobles wanted to acquire exotic foreign goods such as textiles and spices. This increased desire for goods helped establish flourishing trade, and a new group of people was introduced into society: a merchant middle class.

Feudal life was filled with manual labor, as shown in this fifteenth-century French manuscript illustration of peasants building a wattle fence. Fence posts were placed in the ground about six inches apart, and then tree branches were used to "weave" a wall between the posts.

TRADE AND COMMERCE

By the beginning of the twelfth century, many towns had developed along trade routes, while those already in existence prospered further. Some towns grew in size because of their popularity as destinations along pilgrimage routes. All of this activity stimulated local economies.

With the rise of a merchant class, new opportunities for work emerged. Artisans were needed to make the goods to be traded. Bookkeepers, scribes, and clerks were needed for growing businesses. Before long, associations of like-minded workers formed guilds to develop standards of practice within their industries. For example, there were stonemasons' guilds, bakers' guilds, and carpenters' guilds to name a few of the hundreds of such organizations.

Once a guild was formed, its members—masters, journeymen, and apprentices—helped regulate the price and quality of goods. In general, guilds were like the first labor unions. Guild members were given special social and financial support. Artisans could not even practice their craft if they were not guild members. Guild organizations helped provide structure to life in medieval Europe. They provided guidelines for labor such as designated work hours, wages, and work procedures.

Older guild members and their families were even recognized long after a member became too feeble and could no longer work. In cases such as this, a guild member and his family were provided with financial support, food, and in many cases, provisions for those family members who survived the death of a member.

The greatest alliance of guilds occurred in medieval Germany. This group of guilds was called the Hanseatic League and became extremely powerful. Member towns, known as Hanse towns, established trading centers and monopolies across northern Germany. Together the members of the Hanseatic League came to dominate sea trade along the Baltic and North seas. They also kept trading centers in cities such as London. Although other large guild associations dominated regions throughout Europe, the Hanseatic League was the largest and most successful.

Another contributor to the growth of commerce and trade was the traveling pilgrim. Christians from all over Europe routinely traveled to faraway holy cities such as Jerusalem, or more locally to Rome or Canterbury. Others traveled to the shrines and gravesites of Christian martyrs such as the shrine of Saint James in northwestern Spain. Muslims had ruled holy lands for several centuries and allowed Christians to make pilgrimages without prejudice or violence. This was true until conflicts between Muslims and Christians emerged in the eleventh century, sparking a period of unrest between the two groups. In 1095, Pope Urban II incited Christian knights to defend Christianity. For the next 200 years, the Roman Catholic Church supported a series of religious wars known as the Crusades.

Although Christians ultimately failed to regain holy lands from the Muslims, there were benefits to these conflicts. The Crusades brought Christian knights east into the Middle East where they saw firsthand the sophistication and advancements of Muslim culture. Muslim society was better educated, having translated into Arabic many of the classical works of the ancient Greeks and Romans, and they had more experienced scientists, physicians, and architects. Ultimately, the Crusades reopened trade routes from Europe to the Middle East. With that increased trade came European wealth, knowledge, and the cultural exchange of ideas.

In this market scene, a merchant sells a bird to a buyer. Most food, if not grown and raised by consumers, was purchased from area merchants at local markets and fairs. Monk scribes in the Abbey of Monte Cassino in Italy created this image in 1028.

DAILY LIFE

The first medieval towns had begun as self-sufficient villages near castles. The castle walls provided protection and access to communication that was limited during times of invasions. Eventually, medieval towns took a defined shape and had some common characteristics, though most remained individual in appearance. Most contained a town square or common area, narrow winding streets, a church, and a town hall. Many towns had their own wells. Nearby rivers provided power for mills to process grain, to saw wood, or for making cloth or paper. A bell tower marked mass times, the beginning and end of the workday, and nightly curfew. A locked and fortified gate and wall protected the town's citizenry from attack. In some cases, a moat provided extra security. Because of medieval towns' confined design, building was limited. Over time structures became taller, though no building was permitted to be taller than the town church.

Townhomes of the merchant class, many of them two- and three-story structures, were built with protruding upper stories to have more floor space for their growing families. As a result, many three-story structures created shadows over the narrow streets below. Refuse and discarded food littered the streets, and animals such as pigs wandered loose in search of food. Chamber pots and dirty water were usually poured out of opened windows. Smaller, single-story dwellings of peasants had few windows or natural light.

During the early formation of towns, management came from a group of magistrates who had both administrative and judicial duties. Within time, however, as the guild associations became stronger and wielded more power, town merchants dominated governmental decision making. This was especially true in the commercially powerful Italian towns such as Venice. Eventually, the most powerful merchants sought charters from landowners, whether kings, clergy, or other nobles. This allowed them to form a commune and purchase the land on which the town was situated. Once a town's charter was established, its citizens could govern themselves. Citizens of the town were offered certain rights and protections as well as the ability to rent plots of land. It was in this way that medieval towns became more independent. Town leaders could then form laws, develop a system of defense and maintain an army, develop a currency, and levy taxes. Occasionally, however, nobles such as bishops tried to disrupt this process of independence and were often met with rioting and violence from the townspeople.

Life in a Medieval Town

In most cases, medieval towns were established in specific areas along trade routes, near rivers, or near an aspect of a landscape that provided natural protection. (In at least one example, an entire medieval community was built inside a huge, decaying Roman amphitheater.) Walls around the town provided protection and specific entrances for merchants and traders. By controlling who could enter the town, gatekeepers were certain to collect tolls. This income helped support the town's economy.

Town streets were noisy, unpaved, and frequently muddy from flooding. Merchants selling similar items were often found grouped together in sections. For example, the town's butchers were found on one street, while shoemakers or bakers were situated along another. Since most people couldn't read, signs featuring images, not words, hung

Two fortified walls surround the medieval French city of Carcassonne. Located on an ancient border between France and Spain, it had once been a Roman town.

outside the shops. The market square was the center of town and a regular meeting place. The church and town clock were located there. The market square also functioned as a place of public punishments. Farm animals mostly roamed free. The streets were

littered with food scraps and garbage. The worst part of having no system of sanitation was the constant threat of disease.

As a town's population increased, it became more closely knit. It wasn't long before two- and three-story town houses were common. As floors were added, the town houses projected out from the front, nearly touching the structure on the opposite side of the street. This eventually created winding, tunnel-like paths that were increasingly dark and somber.

Merchants used the bottom floor of the town houses as kitchens and to sell goods, while the upper floors provided living space. Rear gardens were where merchant families grew vegetables and herbs as well as raised chickens and pigs. This was also where the outhouse was located, as it was rare for any home to have an indoor bathroom. Fresh water was collected in wooden pails from community wells or streams and would be brought indoors for bathing. Pails of water were also stored outside the home in case of fire, which was a frequent occurrence.

Town House

Imagine what life was like during the Middle Ages by making this authentic replica of a merchant's home and shop.

YOU WILL NEED

- 2 shoeboxes, one larger than the other
- Marker or pen
- Masking tape
- Ruler
- Craft knife
- Scissors
- Glue
- 2 Popsicle sticks
- Cardboard scraps
- Paintbrush
- Brown and white paint
- Brown paper bags
- Glue/water mixture, bowl, brush, and paper strips for papier mâché

Step 1

Measure the bottom length of the larger box (the upper floor) and draw a line in the center dividing it. Draw a window on each half, approximately one inch from the top edge. Carefully cut the windows out using a craft knife. Draw and cut out doorways and windows on the smaller box (the ground floor) as well.

Step 2

Measure the length of the side of your "upper floor" and cut two triangles of that length out of cardboard. Tape the cardboard triangles to each end on the box as shown. Measure the length and width of the front of your box. Cut two pieces of cardboard about ½–inch longer and 1 inch wider than the box. Tape the two pieces together to form a roof. Tape the roof to the triangle ends and along both sides.

Step 3

Glue Popsicle sticks to reinforce the door frame between the windows on the "ground floor" box. Tape both boxes together with masking tape. Insert a piece of cardboard on the lower floor, as shown, to separate the space into

two
rooms.
Dip the paper
strips into the glue/water
mixture. Smooth away excess water
and bubbles with a paintbrush. Cover the
structure with a layer of papier-mâché.

Step 4

After the papier-mâché has fully dried, cut and glue
small strips of cardboard under the overhanging second
floor. Glue strips of cardboard to make support beams,
and frame doorways and windows. Cut small triangles
from cardboard and glue them to round out the
windows, as shown. If desired, reinforce these details
with a layer of papier-mâché.

Step 5

Cut small squares of cardboard to make roof "tiles."
Glue the "tiles" from the bottom of the roof to the top.
Allow time to dry.

Step 6

When completely dry, paint the walls white, the roof
and molding brown, and the interior as you'd like.

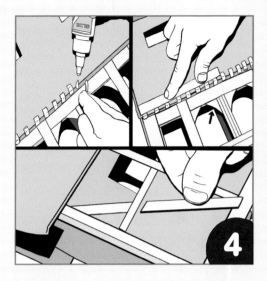

A Shopkeeper's Family

A shopkeeper was considered a member of the middle class. These people were also referred to as burghers, burgesses, or the bourgeoisie. The burgher was likely a master craftsman and had one or two apprentices whom he taught and for whom he provided room and board. He spent his leisure time playing chess, going to fairs, meeting with guild members, drinking beer in the local tavern, and enjoying sports. In general, his middle-class family enjoyed many fine things such as adorned clothing, soft fabrics, and better foods. His family was well cared for and educated.

Although a shopkeeper could rise in his influence, possibly earning a position in local government, he still shared his living space with others. Like the peasant, burghers often shared their shops with another family or at least rented half of it to another craftsman. (Town houses had a staircase only on one side that led to upper floors.)

A typical town house had the store on the lower levels and a solar, or large

Members of nearly every occupation eventually formed guilds. This illustration features various craftspeople at work, including a carpenter, a scribe, and a clockmaker.

hall, on the second floor. The solar was the main living space. It was where the family dined, and it often had a large hearth that provided both heat and lighting. The solar was usually situated next to the kitchen so that both rooms could share warmth and light. A bucket

of water could always be found next to the hearth as well as a variety of kettles and cauldrons. Dried herbs hung from the ceiling, and a garbage pit near the fire held

food waste. The third floor, if there was one, was where the bedrooms were located. Simple wood-framed beds held straw mattresses, woolen blankets, and feather pillows. Bedbugs and lice were a continual problem. The modern bathroom was virtually nonexistent, so people instead made due with chamber pots, pails of water for washing, wooden bathtubs that needed to be filled with heated water manually, and outhouses located in the rear gardens.

The floor was littered with straw, and embroidery hung from the walls. (If a burgher was wealthy enough to have an imported carpet, he usually used it to cover a table. Carpets were considered too fine to walk upon in Europe during the Middle Ages.) Furnishings were minimal. Even a wealthy burgher was limited to only a few items. A long trestle table was used for meals, family members sat upon benches, and cupboards and chests were used to store everyday items such as pots and clothes.

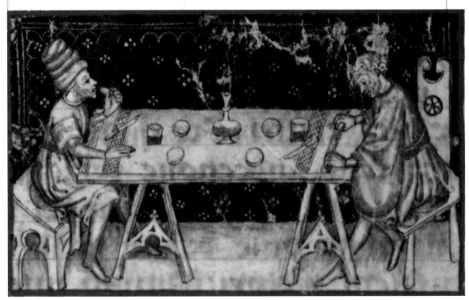

In this fifteenth-century manuscript illustration, two noblemen dine together on a trestle table. Only people of nobility used plates and utensils. Peasants usually placed their food on stale bread called trenchers and ate with their hands.

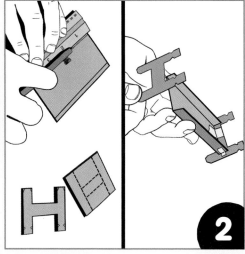

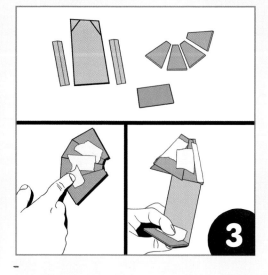

Inside the Town House

Imagine what everyday life was like during the Middle Ages by recreating this interior hearth, bed, and table.

YOU WILL NEED

- Cardboard
- Ruler and pencil
- Scissors and craft knife
- Awl
- Masking tape
- Hay or straw
- Small tree branches
- Self-hardening clay
- Paper clip
- Glue
- Glue/water mixture, bowl, brush, and paper strips for papier mâché
- Paint

Step 1

To make a table, cut two small cardboard rectangles. Cut one of the rectangles in half, making two square pieces for the table legs. Cut a small rectangle into the bottom of both squares. Make a half-inch fold at the top of each square and tape them under your tabletop. Follow the same steps to make a bench.

Step 2

For a bed, cut another rectangle from cardboard, about an inch wider than your table, but just as long. With a ruler and craft knife, score a ½-inch line along the left and right sides of your vertical rectangle. Cut two more squares to make the headboard and baseboard. Cut squares from them to form the letter "H," as shown. Tape these pieces to the front and back of your bed.

Step 3

To make the hearth, cut a rectangle that would fit from floor to ceiling of your interior. Cut the top of the rectangle into a point. This will be the back of your hearth. Cut two strips for the sides, a small rectangle for the base, and four (equal-sized) triangle pieces for

the hearth. Tape the sides of the triangles together to form an arch. Tape the ends to the sides of the pointed back piece. Tape the small rectangle to the bottom of the hearth.

Step 4

Score and fold in half the two side pieces. Tape them to the sides of your hearth. Cover all the pieces in a layer of papier-mâché, as in Step 3 of Project 1. Stand the furniture upright to dry before painting.

Step 5

Once the furniture is painted, use an awl to make a hole in the hearth, just under the hood. Unfold a paper clip and insert it through the hole from the front, exposing a hook. Bend the rest of the clip flat and tape it securely, as shown.

Step 6

Roll two small balls out of clay. To make a kettle, poke a hole in one ball with the end of a paintbrush. Next, cut a paper clip, bend it into an arc, and insert it into one ball. Cut small twigs and insert them into the second ball of clay for the fire.

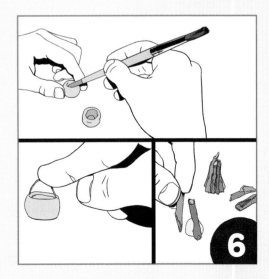

Education in Medieval Europe

Much like it was during ancient times, formal education was a male-dominated institution in the Middle Ages. Even so, few boys gained scholarship opportunities unless they were studying to become priests or take positions in government.

For a noble family in the early Middle Ages, education was private. In the 780s, for example, Charlemagne, king of the Franks, began a small school within his palace at Aachen where English scholars taught his sons and some local youths. When the success of Charlemagne's "school" was evidenced, bishops throughout the empire established small community schools. This system of education was abandoned after Charlemagne's death in 814.

Monasteries, religious centers that were largely isolated, served as centers of learning. Religious clerics and monks were part of an educated minority in western Europe. They were responsible for the maintenance of Europe's only libraries and were often left the challenge of hand-copying important

This fourteenth-century manuscript illustration depicts Charlemagne's coronation to become king of the Franks.

manuscripts such as the Bible and other religious works.

Other centers of learning later included cathedrals. Especially in northern France, established cathedral schools flourished from the late eleventh century onward. These successes eventually gave rise to education on a university level. The first universities were actually guilds, places where

Monks teach small children in this scene from a monastery school in Esslingen, in present-day Germany. Before a permanent school system, monks occasionally taught the children of nobility.

master craftsmen would teach their apprentice students how to re-create their craft on a master level. By the thirteenth century, several universities had become well known, especially in Paris, France, and Bologna and Salerno in Italy.

Male children received a basic education in reading and writing and were often given a hornbook that showcased the alphabet or prayers that they had to memorize. These books, first used in the 1450s, held a single piece of parchment that was sealed on a wooden board with a sheet of horn, a common transparent material made from animal horns that was used in medieval times. Students practiced writing on wax tablets since paper was far too expensive. Other common methods of learning were accomplished through dialogue. In many cases, this meant guessing the answers to riddles.

Hornbooks such as this one from London, England, were used to help teach children before the widespread use of traditional books. This hornbook features the alphabet, vowels, some phonics, and the Lord's Prayer.

Cathedral schools followed a curriculum used by the ancient Romans, which included an emphasis on Latin and grammar. Arithmetic, geometry, astronomy, and music were also offered. Punishment for students who disobeyed or lost interest in their studies was severe.

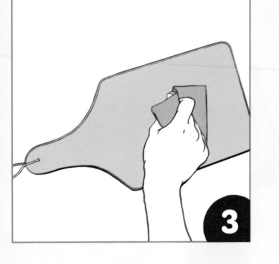

Hornbook

Try your hand at making a medieval hornbook that youngsters hung from their belts and studied to memorize the alphabet or simple prayers.

YOU WILL NEED

- Small wooden cutting board with handle
- Sandpaper
- Brown wood stain
- Acrylic gloss medium
- Paintbrushes
- Paper towels
- Rubber gloves
- Permanent markers
- Ruler
- Pencil
- Drawing paper
- Scissors
- Four thumbtacks

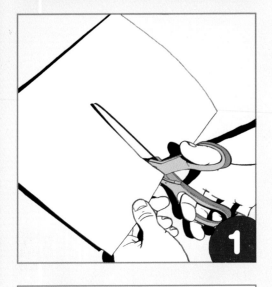

Step 1

Cut a piece of paper to fit in the center of your cutting board. (We used a 14-inch board and our paper was cut to approximately 7 by 4 inches.) The size of your page should be scaled to fit the size of your board.

Step 2

Draw your "medieval" alphabet or text on the drawing paper with a black permanent marker. Use the example pictured here as a guide.

Step 3

Sand the entire cutting board with sandpaper. Sanding will help the wood absorb the stain. Position the alphabet on the board (handle side pointing down) and make a pencil mark on each corner. Remove the paper and set it aside.

Step 4

Using a pencil and ruler, draw a continuous line on the board by connecting the four marks (from Step 3)

to make a frame design. Retrace your lines using a ruler and a brown permanent marker.

Step 5
Place your board on a protected work surface. Follow the instructions on your can of wood stain and wear rubber gloves to protect your skin. Apply the stain with a paintbrush to the board's surface. Wipe away excess stain and set aside to dry.

Step 6
Once dry, apply an acrylic gloss medium to the front of the board. While wet, position the paper alphabet within the drawn lines of your "frame." Cover the paper with acrylic gloss medium to set it in place starting in the center and working your way toward the edges. Use care to avoid air bubbles. Once the acrylic gloss medium has dried, insert thumbtacks into the board to add detail.

The First Banks

T he stability and prosperity of the tenth and eleventh centuries resulted in the increase of trade and commerce. The population was made up of more traders and merchants giving rise to a middle class. With these changes in social order came the need for currency and methods with which to manage the varied currency between kingdoms.

Although coins had been in use for thousands of years, they were not standardized. Nobles in different kingdoms issued a variety of coins with different weights and values. Most of the early European coins were made of silver. At their most varied point during the Middle Ages, more than seventy different currencies were circulating throughout England. Frankish currency was just as diverse, though Charlemagne had introduced a common penny called the denarius that was used widely in local markets. It was also Charlemagne who had introduced a currency system of pounds, shillings, and pence that remained in use in England until 1971.

The banker in this fifteenth-century illustration is using a scale to weigh currency. In the 700s, Charlemagne ordered the first new currency since ancient times, the silver denarius, or penny, on which his portrait was featured. He intended it to be used in local markets for small purchases.

Medieval merchants also often had to act as money changers. Money changers kept a variety of coins in small boxes and used coin balances (scales) to weigh currencies to help determine their value. This system had its disadvantages, as the exchange risked not being fair. Town and city

leaders soon determined that a more universal system of exchange was needed.

It was in Italy that the first merchant banks were fully established. All of the traditional transactions that take place in today's banks, such as keeping accounts, making deposits and withdrawals, exchanging currencies, and securing loans, originated in Italy during the thirteenth century. Records show that eighty banks existed in Florence between 1250 and 1350. Italian merchants were even able to request loans by offering something for collateral, such as armor.

Italian merchants also developed a system of double-entry bookkeeping (where total debts in one account equaled total credits to the other account). In 1252, Florence minted the florin, the first gold coin developed since the height of the Roman Empire. The Venetian ducat followed in 1284. The Venetians were actually the first Europeans to develop a credit system, or a method of lending money. These financial agreements were often started as a way for merchants to lend money to specific trading voyages in order to earn a profit on their investments by charging interest. By the end of the period, banking was an international enterprise.

The gold florin, seen here, was first minted in 1252 and was widely used. The value of the florin grew over time as the price of gold increased.

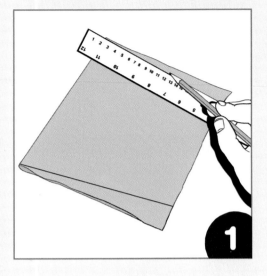

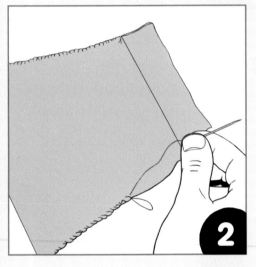

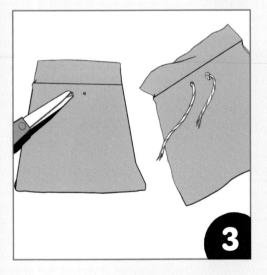

Coins in a Pouch

Create medieval coins and then store them in a velvet pouch that you can wear on your belt like a traveling merchant or trader.

YOU WILL NEED
- 8-inch x 14-inch piece of cloth
- Needle and thread
- Pencil or marker
- Ruler
- Scissors
- String
- Cardboard scraps
- Small round objects to trace
- Aluminum foil

Step 1
Fold the fabric in half like a book with the side you want as the outside of your pouch turned toward the inside. Mark the fabric approximately one inch from the edge on both sides. With a ruler, make diagonal lines from the marked opening to the corners of the fold, as shown.

Step 2
Cut the fabric on the diagonal lines. Remove excess. Draw a line one-inch from the opening as pictured. Sew the two sides, beginning at the fold to the line drawn. Turn the pouch right side out when finished. The part that is not yet sewn will later be folded inward.

Step 3
With your scissors, pinch two tiny holes in the center of the pouch edge, just under the flaps (see illustration). Next, cut a piece of string approximately 21 inches long. Knot one end and thread the string through one hole and out the second hole. Knot the other end of the string to keep it in place.

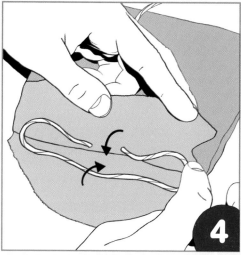

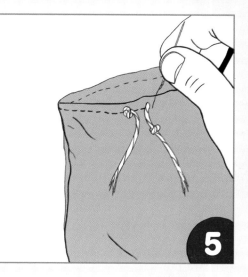

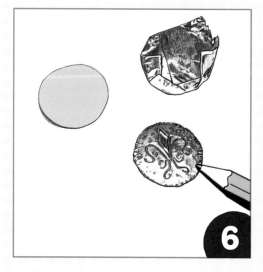

Step 4

Pull the string to form a band along the edge of the pouch opening and fold the flaps over it.

Step 5

Sew a straight line around the outer edge of the bag, trapping the string within the seam. When finished, your pouch should have a working pullstring.

Step 6

To make the coins, trace round flat objects (such as real coins) on pieces of cardboard and cut the circles out. Wrap each disc with a small square of aluminum foil, bending the edges back. On the smooth side of your "coin," press a sharpened pencil into the foil making simple designs on the surface. Examine authentic coins in books to get ideas about what currency looked like during the Middle Ages.

A City Behind Walls

Although commerce depended upon exchanges between places and people, medieval towns (especially those that were not seaports) were often isolated. Defense and security against invaders was paramount. By the late Middle Ages, even the arrival of unarmed strangers could be seen as a threat. The defining event of this period was the spread of the black death (bubonic plague) throughout Europe. This epidemic killed an estimated one-half of western Europe's entire population, causing people in many places to fear and shun outsiders as possible carriers of the contagion.

Town life during the Middle Ages may appear restrictive, but at the time, it was just as likely a source of identity, comfort, and security. People would have lived their entire lives and died within just a few miles of their birthplace. They would have drawn their sense of identity from the village or town where they were born rather than from a larger national identification, such as German or French. For most people,

Towns raised revenue by forcing visitors, like the Flemish merchants in this engraving, to pay a toll upon entering. Because most towns and cities were gated communities with high walls and fortified gates, these taxes were easy to enforce.

their entire life experience took place within a few square miles; they literally knew nothing else.

Since towns were situated behind walled enclosures, tolls could be collected from visitors and guards knew exactly who had entered. Town gates were opened at sunrise and closed at sunset and during times of conflict. The walls

The Grim Reaper is pictured in this idealized manuscript illustration that depicts a scene in a French town during the black death, which ravaged western Europe between 1348 and 1530. Nearly half of the population was eliminated due to the epidemic.

also made the town easier to defend from invaders. Many medieval towns can today be identified by the concentric ring design of their stone walls. As towns expanded, portions of the wall were torn down and then rebuilt to allow more space for housing, gardens, orchards, vineyards, and businesses. In many cases, walls were actually built from the remains of ancient Roman structures. Paris is a good example of a medieval city with a concentric ring design. Towns and cities were also occasionally made even more inaccessible by the addition of a moat surrounding the circular wall on the outside. In addition to having to scale the sides of a stone wall, invaders would have to swim across the moat without being noticed in order to enter.

The twin-towered gatehouse to the eleventh-century Carisbrooke Castle on the Isle of Wight in England is pictured here. This imposing structure was rebuilt in the fourteenth and fifteenth centuries.

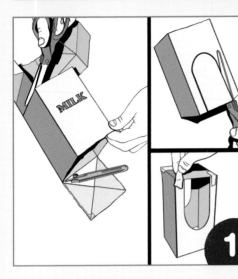

Fortified Gate

Keep tyrants out of town by lifting the ropes on this small model of a fortified gate.

YOU WILL NEED

- 1 half-gallon beverage carton
- 2 pint-sized beverage cartons
- Scrap cardboard
- Masking tape
- Ruler
- Marker
- 35-inch piece of string
- Hole puncher
- 4 small coins
- Scissors
- Craft knife
- Premium craft glue
- Small stones
- Beach or play sand
- Paintbrush
- Craft or acrylic paint

Step 1

With scissors, remove the tops of the cartons. Carefully remove the bottom of the large carton with a craft knife. Draw an arched doorway on one side and cut it out. Use this piece to trace the same size doorway on its opposite side and cut it out, too. Put the cut door pieces aside. Turn the large carton upside down and replace its bottom using masking tape, as shown.

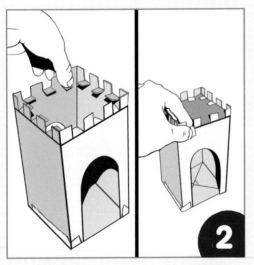

Step 2

Using your ruler and marker, draw a line around each carton approximately ½ inch from the top. With scissors, cut six slits per side, about ½ inch apart, along the perimeter. Fold down alternate tabs, as shown, making crenellations. Next, from scrap cardboard, cut a square the same size as the bottom carton piece in Step 1 and tape it as a roof between the crenellations.

Step 3

With your hole puncher, punch two holes in the large carton over the arch of both the front and back doorways. Punch two additional holes into one of your cut

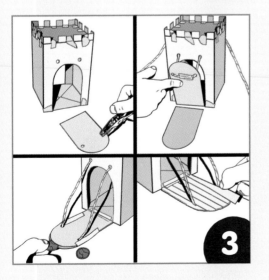

door pieces as shown. These holes should face inward. Tape both door pieces together along the bottom edge and tape to the entrance floor. Thread your string through the holes of the door, and then through the tall carton and out its back. Tape the sides of the doors together and insert a coin before sealing to weigh it down. Cover the door with strips of masking tape, and add strips of cardboard to make horizontal planks.

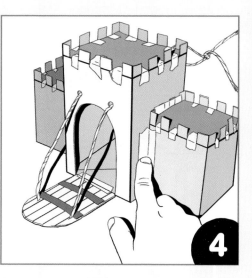

Step 4
Repeat Step 2 to create defense walls out of two pint-sized cartons. Tape the pint cartons to the gatehouse.

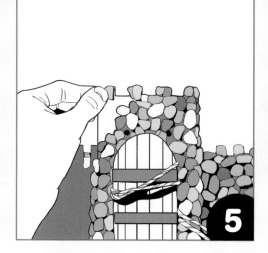

Step 5
Before applying the stones, remove the string. Tip the structure over and spread glue in sections on one side at a time. Press the flat side of the stones into the glue. Before the glue sets, sprinkle sand over the section of stones. (Allow at least thirty minutes to dry.)

Step 6
Sandwich the building between a small stack of books to hold the structure on its side while gluing. Use smaller stones to decorate around the doorway and crenellations. Paint the tops, interior floor, and gate. When completely dry, rethread the strings, tying them together on the reverse side.

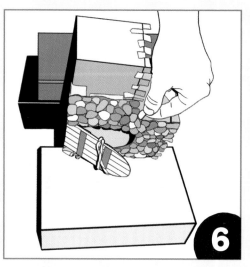

31

After Dark

Two men are beheaded in this illustration from 1377. Capital punishment was common during the Middle Ages, and the means of execution was based on the social ranking of the offender. Nobles were beheaded usually with a limited audience, while peasants were beheaded in front of crowds.

Both petty and serious crimes were committed in medieval towns and cities, though most crimes were kept under control by stiff punishments. Pickpocketing was the most common crime and usually occurred in crowded places such as fairs where people were certain to have coins in their pockets. Most people who were found guilty of a crime were either forced to pay a fine or sentenced to death by hanging or beheading. Stealing was a common occurrence, made worse because begging in the streets was illegal. Since windows were mostly open, or covered with only cloth, entering most town houses was easy. Eventually, wooden shutters that could be closed at night were installed on windows, keeping people and the elements out.

Although a few candles and fires from hearths provided some light along dark, narrow streets, most were pitch black. (Candles were expensive during the Middle Ages and were often reserved for use in churches or cathedrals. The most common types were made from animal fat, which were rather smoky and had a foul odor when burned.) Oil lamps, available since ancient times, were more readily used to provide light. They had wicks made from the pith or core of a single rush plant. Watchmen walked the town at night carrying oil lamps or lanterns. Cheaply made torches helped provide some light around the town's fortress.

Curfews helped limit crime, as people were forced indoors after dark. The term "curfew" originated in France, from the phrase *couvre feu*, or "cover the fire." Cathedral or church bells signaled the end of the day at around eight or nine o'clock. Members of guilds were forced to stop working, and it was illegal to sell any food after sunset. People rushed home, extinguished the hearth (to prevent fires), and often just went to sleep. Without electricity, there was little to do after dark but tell stories.

Merchants, workers, entertainers, and townspeople all interact in this lively street scene from thirteenth-century England. Townspeople had busy days during the Middle Ages, but come sunset, all were forced to retire into their homes and the town gates were locked for safety.

This metal lantern is similar in style to those typically used by night watchmen in the Middle Ages. Despite daily curfews, crimes still took place on town streets, and night watchmen were always on the lookout for suspicious activities.

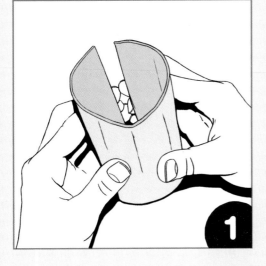

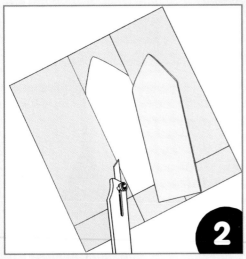

Lantern*

Prepare for the "Dark Ages" by making a replica of a medieval lantern illuminated by a nontoxic light stick.
* ADULT SUPERVISION IS ADVISED FOR THIS CRAFT.

YOU WILL NEED

- Lightweight cardboard
- Oak tag
- Masking tape
- String
- Craft knife
- Hole puncher
- Scissors
- Ruler
- Pencil
- Paper towels
- Black shoe polish
- Yellow light stick

Step 1

Cut out a cardboard rectangle, 7 inches by 7½ inches. Bend and roll the cardboard to form a tube.

Step 2

Flatten the cardboard. Using a ruler and pencil, measure one inch from the bottom. Draw a horizontal line in the center, 1 inch from the bottom, about 2 inches across. Starting from that line, use your pencil and ruler to draw an opening resembling a door about 5 inches high and 2 inches wide. Cut it out and set it aside. Roll the cardboard rectangle back into a tube and tape it closed.

Step 3

Punch two holes along the vertical edge of the cardboard tube opening, as shown. Punch matching holes along the left side of the door. These matching sets of holes will be used to thread string that will hinge the door to the lantern. Make a design in the door by continuing to punch holes in a grid or cross pattern. Set two cardboard circles aside for Step 6.

Step 4

Take a strip of cardboard, 1 inch wide, and make a band. Tape the band closed. Cut small slits along the bottom edge of the band, making flaps. Next, cut a cardboard circle, 2½ inches in circumference. This will be the bottom of your lantern. Tape the flaps of the band to the center of this circle. Next, insert the circle into the bottom of the tube and attach it with tape.

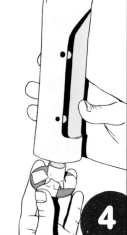

Step 5

Cut an 8-inch piece of string and tie it in a loop to make the handle. Cut a circle out of oak tag, 5 inches in circumference. Cut a 2½-inch slit into the center of the circle and form a cone. Place the knot of the string loop in the center of the cone and twist it to fit. Tape the cone closed. Tape the cone to the top of the lantern.

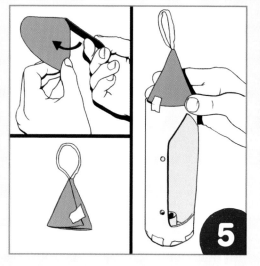

Step 6

Tie the door to the lantern with two small pieces of string. Take the two cardboard circles (from Step 3) and push them back into the two holes along the vertical edge of the cardboard tube where you attached the lantern door. Tape the circles in place from the inside. Cover the entire surface of the lantern with ripped pieces of masking tape. Use your pencil point to puncture the tape through the door to ensure that light can pass through. When completely covered, apply black shoe polish over the entire surface. Next, gently wipe off excess polish.

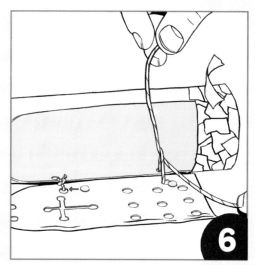

The Medieval Diet

One pig hangs on a spit and another awaits slaughter in this thirteenth-century manuscript illustration featuring a French butcher. Meat was usually salted, smoked, or pickled and could only be frozen during the winter months.

Common misconceptions about the foods Europeans ate during the Middle Ages and how they prepared them remain. For instance, many people believe that medieval cooks prized spices because they were used to disguise the smell or poor taste of rotting meat. This is incorrect. While it is true that storing fresh meat and fish was a challenge without refrigeration, both were preserved using salt. Other preservation methods included smoking, drying, pickling, and packing items in oil.

The medieval diet was one of great variety, made even greater by a person's higher ranking in the social order. For instance, in addition to what was available to anyone, wealthy merchants and noble lords could afford dried and candied fruits, nuts, and expensive spices. Ordinary folk made due with garden vegetables such as onions, leeks, turnips, carrots, wild mushrooms, and a variety of fruits. Beans, local fish, and meat such as rabbit and pork rounded out the standard diet. Pottage was porridge commonly served to the poor. It consisted of grain boiled in water, like rice, and was usually enhanced with flavorful vegetables and beans. The medieval diet also included beer, ale, and wine. Beer provided much-needed carbohydrates for manual laborers.

It is certain that most everyone consumed bread. However, people did

not have ovens in their homes that were hot enough to bake it. The majority of people brought their raw dough to a communal oven, paid a small fee, and had it baked for them while they waited. Because of the high costs of fueling a hot oven (it required a constant supply of wood), communal ovens were an excellent solution. Having a single place to do the baking in the community was actually a lot safer, too. With most buildings made of wood, the outbreak of fire in town was a constant threat. Communal ovens had their drawbacks, however. According to legal records from fourteenth-century London, some bakers had a habit of stealing bits of every customer's loaf, eventually having enough to make a hodgepodge loaf of their own!

Bread*

Most people lacked plates during the Middle Ages. Instead, people often set their food on trenchers, which were flat, mostly stale breads formed in the shape of crude discs. By combining the ingredients to form basic bread, we've adapted this recipe so you too can make your own bread "plates."

* ADULT SUPERVISION IS ADVISED FOR THIS CRAFT.

YOU WILL NEED

- 4 cups whole wheat flour
- 1 tablespoon sugar
- ½ tablespoon baking powder
- ½ tablespoon baking soda
- 1½ cups water
- 2 tablespoons apple cider vinegar
- Baking sheet
- A floured work surface
- ⅓ stick of melted butter (for glaze)
- Brush

Step 1
Preheat your oven to 350 degrees. Combine the dry ingredients in a large bowl and mix. Set aside.

Step 2
In a measuring cup, combine the water and apple cider vinegar (white vinegar can be used as a substitute). Add the wet ingredients to the large bowl and mix well with your hands to form sticky dough.

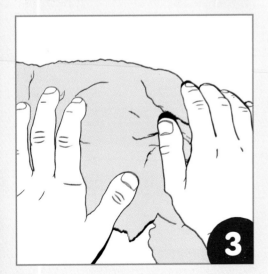

Step 3
Turn the dough out onto a floured work surface (wood or marble is best). Knead the dough for two to four minutes. Do not overwork it. If your work surface becomes too sticky, sprinkle it with flour as needed.

Step 4

Shape your dough into 5-inch discs. This recipe yields five to six discs. You can fit about three 5-inch discs on an ungreased baking sheet.

Step 5

Place the baking sheet in the center rack of your oven and bake your discs for 25 to 30 minutes or until they are golden brown.

Step 6

When you are satisfied with the color of your trenchers, carefully remove the pan using potholders. Ask an adult for help if you are not sure if your bread is fully cooked. Remove the discs from the pan and place them on wire racks to cool. Melt the butter in a small saucepan on the stovetop. While the trenchers are still hot, coat them with a butter glaze to give them added flavor.

Art and Recreation

During the Middle Ages, leisure activities were enjoyed by the masses. Some, such as falconry and hunting, were available only to nobles. Dancing, playing card games, and listening to music were just some of the activities enjoyed by everyone. Games of reason, such as telling riddles or playing guessing games, were also popular. Because of a lack of literacy, the memorization of riddles was a form of entertainment.

Sports such as archery, a form of tennis, swimming, and ice-skating were also common. Most people played chess and knucklebones, a game that originated in the ancient world and is similar to jacks. Gambling was first commonly done with dice. Then, during the late Middle Ages when cards were invented, people usually bet on the outcome of the card games. (Gambling was, in fact, among the vices that magistrates tried repeatedly to outlaw.) Other forms of entertainment included betting on the outcome of animal fights, attending public executions and punish-

The Frenchman in this manuscript illustration has a falcon on his hand. Falconry was a sport enjoyed during the Middle Ages by nobility and clergy, both of whom used the birds to assist them while hunting.

ments, and jousting (combat), which could also result in injury or death.

Live entertainment was among the most popular activities. Noble families enjoyed talented storytellers, poet troubadours, and musicians such as minstrels. Musicians played a variety of instruments of the day including the lute, guitar, gittern (a stringed

Florentines take part in a soccer game in this painting by Italian artist Giorgio Vasari. Many sports that are popular today were also enjoyed during the medieval period. People of all ages adored entertainment and loved group activities.

instrument), violin-like instruments, and the psaltery, which was plucked, not strummed. Wind instruments such as flutes and trumpets were also played. Often, common people would hear music, storytelling, and poetry only during feasts or festivals, though many of the performers in these events were local amateurs.

Town guilds staged plays, especially to illustrate religious themes during feast days and holidays. For example, the Easter season was often a time to perform passion plays. By contrast, the twelve days of Christmas celebration, which took place between December 25 and January 6, usually featured a variety of feasts and public performances. Sometimes the twelve-day feast was an excuse to celebrate excessively. Public celebrations of this sort also welcomed puppet shows, acrobats, jugglers, animal trainers with playful dogs or "dancing" bears, and pantomime players, who performed in silence.

The woman gazing out from this painting is playing a psaltery, a medieval stringed instrument that was popular since ancient times. Music was enjoyed by all social classes and was played in the streets, during fairs and celebrations, and in cathedrals and churches.

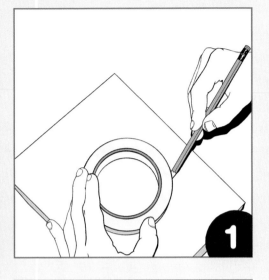

Psaltery

Transform a gift box into a medieval instrument called a psaltery.

YOU WILL NEED

- A heavy-weight flat cardboard box with matching lid
- Cardboard
- Medium-sized rubber bands
- Masking tape
- Paper
- Pencil
- Scissors
- Craft knife
- Hole puncher
- Glue
- Paint and paint brush

Step 1

Place a roll of masking tape onto the center of your box top and trace the outline as shown. Carefully cut out the circle with a craft knife.

Step 2

Cover the surface of your box top with strips of masking tape to resemble wooden panels. Cut slits into the tape to fold around the edge of the circular opening, as shown.

Step 3

On a piece of paper, trace the same sized circle as you did in Step 1. Carefully cut outside the circle you just drew, allowing for a ½-inch border along its circumference. Next, fold the circle in half and continue folding until you have a cone shape. Draw a simple design on the cone, as pictured. Cut the design out of the cone with scissors as you would to make a paper snowflake. Add additional details by using a hole puncher.

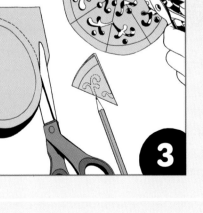

Step 4

Position your circle on the interior of the box top, covering the hole, and tape it in place. Next, cut two

strips of cardboard the length of your box, but ½-inch larger in width. Cut ½-inch slits, about 1 inch apart, along one side of each cardboard strip. Make matching slits along the bottom of both sides of your box lid, as shown. Glue the strips to the sides of your box top, lining up the slits on the strips with the ones along the bottom edge of the box.

Step 5
Once the glue has dried, paint the entire box, painting in the direction of the tape strips. Gently paint the paper center to avoid breakage.

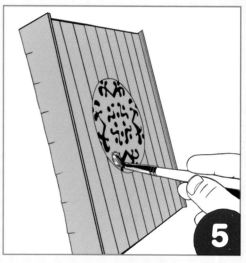

Step 6
Once your box is dry, stretch rubber bands around the lid and wedge them into the cardboard slits on the bottom. Carefully pull the bands tighter to make a higher pitch when strummed. Before putting the box back together, remove the long sides of the bottom part. Attach the top to the bottom of the box by inserting the uncut sides into the lid, as shown. Now you're ready to play a medieval melody.

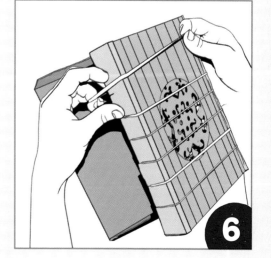

TIMELINE

AD 313	Constantine imposes the Edict of Milan, preaching tolerance for Christianity.
410	Visigoths sack Rome.
circa 476	The Roman Empire falls.
476–1000	The period historians sometimes refer to as Europe's Dark Ages.
circa 700	Feudal system is established in France.
711	Muslims invade Spain.
768	Charlemagne becomes king of the Franks.
793	Beginning of Viking raids in England.
1066	William the Conqueror conquers England.
1095	Pope Urban II urges Christian knights to defend Christianity.
1096–1291	The Christian Crusades are launched to recapture the Holy Land from Muslims.
1161	First guilds are established; the era of cathedral-building begins.
1171	The Bank of Venice opens.
1179	The third Lateran Council decrees all cathedrals must have schools.
1180	Windmills first appear in Europe.
1215	The fourth Lateran Council requires Jews to wear identifying badges; signing of the Magna Carta.
1241	Mongols invade Europe.
1271	Marco Polo travels to Asia.
1300	Feudalism ends.
1314–1322	The great famine (alternate droughts and heavy rains in northern Europe).
1337–1453	Hundred Years' War between England and France.
1347–1530	The plague kills about 25 million people throughout Europe.
1381	Peasants' Revolt.
1453	The fall of Constantinople to Ottoman Turks (often taken as end of Middle Ages).

GLOSSARY

apprentice A young person who studies under a master artisan in order to learn a specific craft.

bishop A church leader serving under the pope.

charter A written agreement or contract that outlined a town's area, its privileges, and its authority to collect tolls and taxes and begin an independent system of government.

Crusades A series of religious wars between Christians and Muslims that occurred during the Middle Ages beginning in 1096.

Dark Ages A period in European history after the fall of the Roman Empire, between 476 and 1000, when people were increasingly isolated because of fear of invasion and political instability.

feudalism A political and social system established during the Middle Ages.

guild An organization or group of like-minded individuals who regulated a particular industry.

kingdom A territory or community ruled over by a monarch.

knight A man-at-arms who served a feudal superior.

lord A male knight and/or noble who was given a fief by the king and who lived at a large estate or castle that provided for himself, his family, and his servants and their families.

magistrate A political official who administered the laws of a town after it was made independent through a charter agreement.

master An artisan who is a member of a guild and is expertly skilled in a specific craft.

Middle Ages A period of time in western Europe between the fall of the Roman Empire in 476 and the beginning of the Renaissance in 1450.

monastery A complex of buildings that usually included a church and housed monks.

pilgrimage A journey made to a religious site or a holy city such as Jerusalem.

principality The territory of a prince.

FOR MORE INFORMATION

The Cloisters
Fort Tryon Park
New York, NY 10040
e-mail: cloisters@metmuseum.org
Web site: http://www.metmuseum.org

The Metropolitan Museum of Art
1000 Fifth Avenue
New York, NY 10028-0198
(212) 535-7710
Web site: http://www.metmuseum.org

WEB SITES

Due to the changing nature of Internet links, the Rosen Publishing Group, Inc., has developed an online list of Web sites related to the subject of this book. This site is updated regularly. Please use the link below to access the list:

http://www.rosenlinks.com/ccma/meto

FOR FURTHER READING

Chrisp, Peter. *Town and Country Life* (Medieval Realms). San Diego, CA: Lucent Publishers, 2004.

Corbishley, Mike. *The Middle Ages* (Cultural Atlas for Young People). New York, NY: Facts on File, 2003.

Gies, Joseph, and Frances Gies. *Life in a Medieval City*. New York, NY: Harper Perennial, 1981.

Hanawalt, Barbara A. *The Middle Ages: An Illustrated History* (Oxford Illustrated Histories YA). New York, NY: Oxford University Press, 1999.

Hart, Avery, Paul Mantell, and Michael Kline. *50 Hands-On Activities to Experience the Middle Ages* (Kaleidoscope Kids). Charlotte, VT: Williamson Publishing, 1998.

INDEX

A

artisans, 9

B

bakers, 37
beer, 36
bookkeeping, 25
bubonic plague, 28

C

candles, 32
carpets, 17
cathedrals, 20, 32, 33
Catholic(ism), 5–6, 8, 10
Charlemagne, 20, 24
Christmas, 41
crime, 32, 33
Crusades, 8, 10
curfew, 11, 33

E

Easter, 41

F

fairs, 8, 32

farming/agriculture, 6, 7–8
feudalism, 6–7
fire(s), 13, 32, 33, 37
furniture, 17

G

gambling, 40
guilds, 9, 11, 16, 21, 33, 41

H

Hanseatic League, 9

I

Islam/Muslims, 5, 8, 9–10

L

Latin, 6, 21
libraries, 20

M

merchants, 8, 11, 24, 36
middle class, 8, 16, 24
monasteries, 20
music/musicians, 21, 40–41

O

outhouse(s), 13, 17

P

pilgrims, 9
pope, power of, 6, 7
population, 8, 13

R

Renaissance, 4
Roman Empire, 4–5, 7, 25

S

sanitation, 13
solar, 16

T

trade, 5, 8, 9, 10, 12, 24

U

universities, 20–21
Urban II (pope), 10

V

Vikings, 5, 8

ABOUT THE AUTHOR AND ILLUSTRATOR
Joann Jovinelly and Jason Netelkos have collaborated on many educational projects for young people. This is their second crafts series encouraging youngsters to learn history through hands-on projects. Their first series, Crafts of the Ancient World, was published by the Rosen Publishing Group in 2001. They live in New York City.

PHOTO CREDITS
Cover (center), p. 33 (bottom) © Dorling Kindersley; p. 4 © Historical Picture Archive/Corbis; p. 5 Courtesy of the University of Texas Libraries, The University of Texas at Austin; p. 7 The Art Archive/Biblioteca Bertoliana Vicenza/Dagli Orti; p. 8 The Art Archive/British Library; pp. 10, 13 (top), 24, 41 (top) Scala/ Art Resource, NY; p. 12 © Jonathan Blair/Corbis; p. 13 (bottom) © John Heseltine/ Corbis; p. 16 The Art Archive/Bibxlioteca Estense Modena/Dagli Orti; p. 17 (top) © Geoff Dann/Dorling Kindersley; p. 17 (bottom) permission British Library [Harley 3448]; pp. 20, 25 (top), p. 37 (bottom) akg-images; p. 21 (top) Bildarchiv Preussischer Kulturbesitz/Art Resource, NY; p. 21 The Granger Collection, New York; p. 25 (bottom) © Archivo Iconografico, S.A./Corbis; pp. 28, 33 (top) © Mary Evans Picture Library/The Image Works; p. 29 (top) Bibliotheque Nationale, Paris, France, Giraudon/Bridgeman Art Library; p. 29 (bottom) © Justin Kase/ Alamy; p. 32 © C. Walker/Topham/The Image Works; pp. 36, 40 The Art Archive/ Real Biblioteca de lo Escorial/Dagli Orti; p. 37 (top) The Art Archive/Bibliotheque Municipale Valenciennes/Dagli Orti; p. 41 (bottom) © Sandro Vannini/Corbis. All craft illustrations, photographs and crafts by Jason Netelkos. Craft photography by Joann Jovinelly.

Designer: Evelyn Horovicz; Editor: Leigh Ann Cobb
Photo Researcher: Nicole DiMella